Milly, Moll
Blind Bertie

"We may look different
but we feel the same."

Milly and Molly wriggled up on to the park
bench beside Blind Bertie.

"Good morning," he said. "Have you come to
find peace and joy?"

"Who are peace and joy?" asked Milly and
Molly.

"If you can sit quietly long enough to note the things that make you smile, you'll find peace and joy," said Blind Bertie.

"We can sit quietly long enough," said Milly and Molly.

At first they were dazzled by the hustle and
bustle of the city.

Then, very slowly, the big sights and sounds
disappeared and the small ones came in to
view.

A small white daisy held its face to the sun
from a crack in the concrete.

A mother duck proudly waddled her way to the pond

and a blackbird scuffed for worms.

A little dog ran by with a shoe

and a cat moved her kitten to a safer home.

An old man soaked up the sunshine

and two old ladies sipped tea and remembered.

A mother was lost in her world

and a father strode out to keep up.

Three yellow balloons found freedom

and a feather played on the wind.

A butterfly tiptoed and danced

while an ant marched off with a crumb.

Milly and Molly had sat long enough.
Catching oak leaves with friends was more
than they could resist.

When they were exhausted they wriggled up
again beside Blind Bertie.
"Did you find peace and joy?" he asked.

"We were quiet long enough and we smiled,"
said Milly.
"There," rejoiced Blind Bertie, "you found
peace and joy."

"You can't see, Blind Bertie," said Molly softly.
"How do you find peace and joy?"

"I feel it in the sunshine and I hear it in the laughter," he said.